Emmy
the Exaggerating Elephant

Fenton
the Fearful Frog

Gertie
the Grungy Goat

the Happy Hamster

the Impatient Iguana

Ollie
the Obedient Ostrich

Perry
the Polite Porcupine

Queenie
the Quiet Quail

Rupert
the Resourceful Rhinoceros

Wendy
the Wise Woodchuck

Xavier
the X-ploring Xenops

Yori
the Yucky Yak

Ziggy
the Zippy Zebra

NOTE TO PARENTS

<u>Una Cheers Us Up</u>
A story about self-acceptance

In this story, Una the Unhappy Unicorn is convinced that her horn is nothing but a hindrance until she finds out how members of her family have put their horns to good and creative use over the years. Once aware of this, she comes to terms with her special attribute and learns to appreciate her uniqueness.

In addition to enjoying this story with your child, you can use it to teach a gentle lesson about making the most of your natural attributes and appreciating individual differences in yourself and others.

You can also use this story to introduce the letter **U**. As you read about Una the Unhappy Unicorn, ask your child to listen for all the words that start with **U** and point to the objects that begin with **U**. Explain that the letter **U** is a vowel and has more than one sound. When you've finished reading the story, your child will enjoy doing the activity at the end of the book.

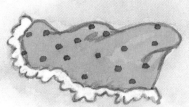

The AlphaPets™ characters were conceived and created by Ruth Lerner Perle.
Characters interpreted and designed by Deborah Colvin Borgo.
Cover/book design and production by Norton & Company.
Logo design by Deborah Colvin Borgo and Nancy S. Norton.

Printed and Manufactured in the United States of America

Una
Cheers Us Up

RUTH LERNER PERLE

Illustrated by Judy Blankenship

Grolier Enterprises Inc.,   Danbury, Connecticut

One foggy morning, Una the Unhappy Unicorn was getting dressed. When she pulled her new blue sweater over her head, her horn got stuck in the sleeve.

Una pulled and pulled. Then, *rrrip!* Her horn tore through the sleeve.

"This dumb horn is always in the way!" Una grumbled. "Now I'll have to mend my new sweater."

Una looked in her sewing box, but she didn't have the right color thread. "I'll go next door to Connie's house. She must have some blue thread," Una thought. But as she turned to close the door behind her, her horn caught in the door hinge. Una tripped and fell.

"Ouch!" she cried. "It's that dumb horn *again*!"

Connie the Cuddly Cat was looking out of her window and saw what happened to Una. She rushed over to help.

"I'm the unluckiest person in the world!" cried Una.

"Oh, Una, anyone can have an accident," Connie said.

"But accidents always seem to happen to me. And it's all because of my dumb horn," complained Una.

Just then Ollie the Obedient Ostrich came by with Perry the Polite Porcupine who was pulling his wagon.

"Good morning, Una!" Perry said.

"It doesn't seem so good to me!" Una grumbled. "It looks foggy and awful!"

"You seem upset. Is there anything I can do to help you?" Ollie asked.

"Nothing can help me," Una mumbled, and she began to cry.

"I know something that will cheer you up!" Perry said. "We're going to ride my wagon down Hayride Hill. Why don't you and Connie come along?"

"Not today," Una said. "I feel too unhappy. Besides, my horn would probably get in the way and spoil the fun."

Una said good-bye to her friends. She ran into her house and forgot all about the thread.

"I'll come along with you," Connie said to Perry and Ollie. "But I wish Una were coming, too."

Una went to her bedroom and looked in the mirror. "Everything would be all right if I didn't have this dumb horn," she said to herself. "It always gets in the way, it causes accidents, and it's ugly."

Then Una had an idea. "Maybe if I wrap it up, my horn won't get stuck on everything," she thought.

So Una climbed up the stairs to the attic to look for something to wrap her horn with.

Una pushed the attic door open and looked around. The attic was crowded with barrels, boxes, and baskets full of all kinds of unique and unusual things.

She stepped inside and walked past an old upright piano. Suddenly, *crash!* Her horn bumped against a wall and sent a box of umbrellas clattering to the floor.

"This dumb horn!" Una cried. As she put the umbrellas back, Una noticed an old ukelele leaning against the wall. She picked it up and strummed a few chords.

"I remember when Uncle Ulver played this ukelele," she said to herself. "It always made me feel better when he strummed his old tunes. Uncle Ulver always seemed happy. He had a horn, just like mine, but it never seemed to get in *his* way."

Una put the ukelele down and continued to look for something to wrap her horn in. She was rummaging through some things in an old steamer trunk when she felt something hard near the bottom. She pulled it up so she could see what it was.

There, all covered with dust, was a big, old family photo album!

Una blew the dust off the album and opened it carefully. The first page had a picture of Uncle Ulysses wearing a bright red and gold uniform. He was leading a parade, and there was a flag proudly waving from his magnificent horn.

"He looks wonderful!" Una whispered to herself.

Una turned the page. There was Aunt Ursula, the photographer, taking underwater pictures. She had a flashlight attached to her horn to help her see.

"What a good idea!" Una thought.

There were more pictures.

GRANDMA UNICORN
KNITTING

GRANDPA UNICORN
PAINTING THE CEILING

COUSIN URSA
AS MAYPOLE
QUEEN

THE YOUNG UNICORN COUSINS PLAYING RING TOSS

COUSIN UPTON GETTING A KITE OUT OF A TREE

COUSIN URIAH IN HIS BAGEL BAKERY

"Oh, wow! This is great! This is unbelievable! It's stupendous!" Una shouted, dancing around the room. "Look at all the marvelous, useful, terrific things a unicorn horn can do!"

Una returned the album to the trunk. "Maybe I don't need to cover my horn after all," she said, and she skipped down the stairs.

Back in her room, Una looked in the mirror again, but this time her horn didn't seem ugly at all.

Una smiled a happy smile. "Maybe I can find a good use for *my* horn, too," she said to herself. "But for now, I'll surprise everybody and meet them after all. We'll have fun riding in Perry's wagon."

Una took a last admiring look in the mirror. For the first time, she liked what she saw. Instead of hiding her horn, she wanted everyone to notice it.

Then Una spotted a bright pink sash hanging in her closet. She took it off the hook and tied it on her horn in a big floppy bow. "There!" she said with a smile. "That's perfect."

It was very foggy when Una left the house, but she
didn't mind at all.

"What's a little fog when the sun shines in your
heart?" she thought.

So, humming a happy tune, Una skipped and hopped
all the way to Hayride Hill.

By the time Una arrived at Hayride Hill, the fog was thicker than ever. She looked everywhere, but the AlphaPets were nowhere to be seen.

Suddenly, Una saw Perry's wagon lying upside down at the bottom of the hill. "Perry! Perry!" Una called. But there was no answer. Una looked up the hill, but she could hardly see anything. She paced back and forth, wondering what to do next.

Ollie, Perry, and Connie had been riding down the hill in Perry's wagon all morning. Then the fog became so thick that their wagon bumped into a tree. They fell out, and the wagon rolled away from them. Now the three friends were trying to find their wagon and their way down the hill.

"Oh, dear," Perry cried. "If it doesn't clear up, we'll be stuck here forever."

Suddenly they heard Una calling. Perry squinted his eyes and saw something pink moving back and forth through the fog. It looked like a bow, and it seemed to be tied to a horn.

"Look down there!" Perry said. "I think that's Una!"

"Hurray!" Ollie cried. "Now, if we could only get to where Una is, we'll be safe."

Hand-in-hand the three AlphaPets walked down the side of the hill, keeping their eyes on Una's horn.

When they were finally at the bottom, Connie, Perry, and Ollie went running over to Una.

"Oh, Una!" Connie said. "Thank heavens for your horn. We followed the bow so we could find our way!"

"I'm so glad I could help you. I guess a horn is a pretty good thing to have after all," said Una. "But we'd better hurry home now. The fog is getting worse and worse."

Una lead everybody safely back to her house and invited them in.

The AlphaPets looked tired and cold.

"You'd better get out of your muddy clothes and warm up around the fire," Una said in a cheery voice. "I'll bring you a nice snack while you change."

Una brought a plate full of cookies and four mugs of steaming hot chocolate. Then she stoked the fire and looked around at the AlphaPets. They were munching away, but they still didn't seem to be very happy.

Una had an idea. "I know just what will make you feel better!" she exclaimed. She rushed up the attic steps, and a few minutes later returned with the ukelele.

Una struck a chord, then another, and another.

Soon Perry, Ollie, and Connie began to smile and tap their feet. And before long, they were laughing and singing and dancing.

Then Connie gave Una one of her cuddliest hugs and said, "If it weren't for that wonderful horn of yours, we'd probably still be lost."

"Yes," Perry added. "Thank you so very much for helping us!"

"And for cheering us up!" Ollie added.

The AlphaPets held up their mugs and shouted, "You're special, Una! Cheers to you, and to your very special horn!"

Have fun learning these words with me.

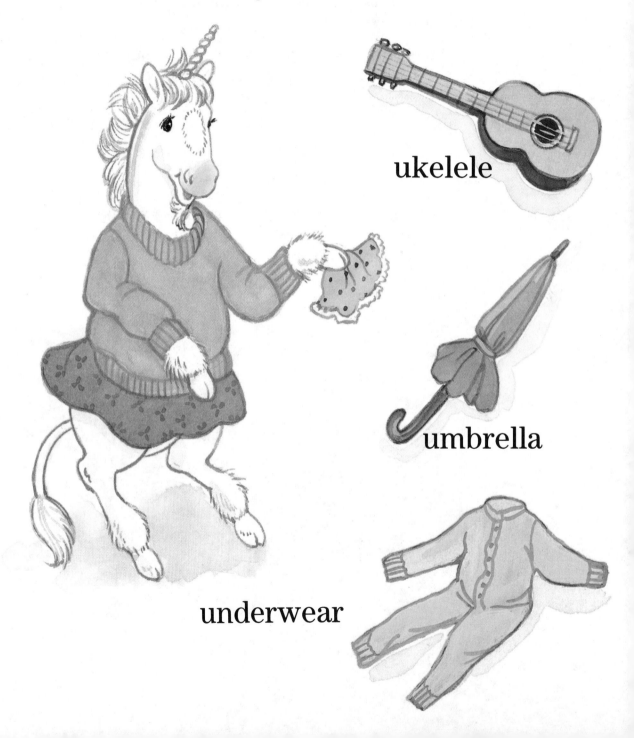

ukelele

umbrella

underwear

uniform

umpire

unicycle

Look back at the pages of this book and try to find these and other words that start with U.

Aa Bb

Gg Hh

Mm Nn Oo Pp

Uu Vv Ww